WALT DISNEY'S
BAMBI

A Golden Book · New York

Western Publishing Company, Inc.
Racine, Wisconsin 53404

It happened on a soft spring day. A little prince was born in the forest.

The little prince was a deer. He had wobbly legs. He had sleepy eyes. His name was Bambi.

Soon Bambi's legs weren't so wobbly and his eyes weren't so sleepy. Thumper the rabbit came and began to thump on a hollow log with his foot.

"Come and play with me!" called Thumper happily.

So Bambi played with Thumper. When Thumper jumped over a log, Bambi jumped over the log, too. At least, he tried to jump over it.

Bambi also played with Thumper's
brothers and sisters. They slid down
a big hill.

He played with Flower the skunk.
They sniffed at some daisies.

A butterfly floated down on a sunbeam and sat on Bambi's tail.

A mother quail hurried past with her babies. "Hello, Bambi!" cried the quail babies.

A mother bluebird perched beside her nest. "Good morning, Bambi!" the little bluebirds chirped.

Summer came, and Bambi knew
Flower and Thumper and the birds
and the chipmunks and the squirrels
—but he never saw another little deer.

The day came when Bambi's mother led him far away from the thicket where he had been born. She led him to a place where the trees ended.

"This is the meadow," she said.

It was wide and green. It was open and free. And, for the first time, Bambi saw other deer.

One was a young deer. She was a
baby, like Bambi himself.

"This is Faline," Bambi's mother
told him.

Faline laughed and ran away, and
Bambi started to run after her.
"Stop!" cried Bambi's mother.

Bambi stood very still. There was a great stag in the meadow. The stag came to Bambi and looked him over carefully. Then the stag went on into the forest.

"Why did he look at me?" asked Bambi.

His mother said, "He is the Great Prince of the Forest, Bambi. He is your father."

Summer ended, and the wind blew
chill. One morning there was ice on
the pond.

Thumper liked the ice. "Come and
slide!" he called. "The water's stiff!"

"It's winter," Flower the skunk decided. "All flowers go to sleep in the wintertime."

So Flower said good night. Then she crept into a cozy cave and fell sound asleep.

After that, Bambi didn't see Flower, and he didn't see the birds. The woods were silent and lonely.

"Never mind. Spring will come," said his mother. "It always does."

Spring did come. The trees blossomed, and the birds came back. Then Flower woke up and smiled at the warm sun.

The ice on the pond melted, and
Bambi looked at himself in the water.
He did not see a baby deer. He saw a
young stag with brave new antlers.

Best of all in that happy new spring, Bambi saw Faline. She, too, wasn't a baby deer any longer. She was a young doe, very pretty, and this time she didn't laugh or run away.

Of course, she wouldn't, for Bambi was the young Prince of the Forest.